JEANNE

THE DEAD GIRL IN A LACE DRESS

Happy Birthday Silke!

Martina

Peter

Also published by Edinburgh University Press

Waterweed in the Wash-houses
by Jeanne Hyvrard
Jeanne Hyvrard: Theorist of the Modern World
by Jennifer Waelti-Walters

JEANNE HYVRARD: THE DEAD GIRL IN A LACE DRESS

Translated by
J.-P. Mentha
&
J. Waelti-Walters

EDINBURGH UNIVERSITY PRESS

Edinburgh University Press
22 George Square
Edinburgh EH8 9LF

Typeset in Caslon by
Pioneer Associates Ltd., Perthshire
and printed and bound in
Great Britain

A CIP record of this book is available
from the British Library

ISBN 0 7486 0821 4

CONTENTS

INTRODUCTION
Jennifer Waelti-Walters
1

THE DEAD GIRL
IN A LACE DRESS
7

INTRODUCTION

Jeanne Hyvrard was born in Paris in 1945, the third child in a middle-class family. She studied economics, married a fellow economics student and with him lived for some time in Martinique before returning to Paris in the early 1970s. They have one daughter who is an engineer. Hyvrard herself teaches political economy in a technical high school in Paris.

Jeanne Hyvrard (a pseudonym chosen to preserve the memory of an aunt expunged from the family) began to be published in 1975. *The Dead Girl in a Lace Dress* (1990) is her twelfth book.[1] Its subject connects back closely to one of the main themes of her first novel, *Les Prunes de Cythère* (The Plums of Cythera), that of an unsatisfactory mother-daughter relationship. In *Les Prunes*, the oppression of a daughter by her mother is only one of many layers of colonisation. In fact, to this day, Hyvrard claims that the novel is a report on the economic situation of Martinique, and so it is, but not in the terms of traditional economics. The text includes many strands of information that are excluded from usual economic analysis because they are non-quantifiable: the situation of women and children, effects of colonisation, rebellion, poverty. Hyvrard included those and produces 'chaos economics', in the sense that chaos theory uses the word. Her writing style also is what I term 'chaos writing', rather than simple stream-of-consciousness or *l'écriture féminine*. The various themes run together, combine and recombine in ways that produce knowledge in an intuitive or pre-rational form. (Hyvrard calls such knowledge 'encepts', as opposed to concepts which are fixed and definable.) She writes the world in process. This is one of the major distinctions between her writing and that of Hélène Cixous. Cixous writes out from her own body in quest of the unnameable in the female experience. Hyvrard also writes out from her own body, and her thought is in many ways comparable to that of Luce Irigaray, but she draws parallels from the female body to the body politic on the social and global scale.

In *Les Prunes* Hyvrard establishes themes which she explores through her subsequent novels. One is the increasing economic, political and ecological devastation of the post-colonial world, which is the central focus of *Le Corps défunt de la comédie* (The Corpse of the Comedy, 1982), *Canal de la Toussaint* (All Saints Canal, 1985), and *Ton nom de végétal* (Your Vegetable Name, 1996). A second theme is the search for any trace of a lost female genealogy reaching back to the chaos before the Creation as described in the Bible. This is the main topic of *Mère la mort* (Mother Death, 1976), Hyvrard's second novel, and of the twin texts published in 1977: *Les Doigts du figuier* (The Fingers of the Fig-tree) and *La Meurtritude* (Waterweed in the Wash-houses).[2]

Hyvrard is searching for a language to express thought processes that are rooted in awareness of non-separation, rather than the rational thought processes rooted in the taxonomies of pragmatism, logic and science. She calls the former 'woman thought', 'round thought', 'fusional thought' and 'body thought' at various times in her writing. *La Pensée corps* (Body Thought, 1989) is a cross-referencing, non-definitional dictionary of women's experience in process as Hyvrard describes it. *La Pensée corps* together with *Canal de la Toussaint* present and illustrate her philosophy and view of the world.

The three themes come together explicitly in Hyvrard's writing on cancer. In *Le Cercan* (1987) she explores the devouring of cancer patients by the medical system, and in *Ton nom de végétal* the devastation of body, spirit and planet by chemical pollution, and the difficulty in separating what is toxic from what is healing. Hyvrard attributes her own cancer to a failure of love. There is a conversation between her and her mother in *Le Cercan* where they discuss her mother's uterine cancer and Hyvrard's breast cancer in this context. The damage created by a non-loving relationship between mother and child is developed in a different way in *The Dead Girl*. Here the metaphor is not disease but bonsai-sation: the deliberate restriction of life to the minimum. The mother is seen to devour the child's potential, to constrict all activity, mental or physical, to turn all nurture into deprivation, with her continued response 'There's not . . .'.

Dead Girl in a Lace Dress is not written in the same style as the other books. It is the only one that has been written directly on the computer (Hyvrard said she needed that distancing in order to explore her topic at all), and it is the only one which does not overtly link the personal to the global. It is, however, written out from the female body, taking the physical circumstances, constraints and sensations of her narrator as the touchstone of what she has to say. The situation is one of 'abjection' as defined by Julia Kristeva.[3]

The focus in *The Dead Girl* is on the relationship between a mother and her youngest daughter. The child, who varies in age between about four years old and adolescence, is increasingly aware that she has no sense at all of herself as an individual. There is always 'some Mummy' between herself and her dealings with the world. This 'Mummy' is a sticky substance that oozes into everything: between the child and her clothes, under her skin, even inside her digestive tract. Annie sets out to discover and understand how this can be. She proceeds by isolating and analysing individual incidents in her life and by examining her mother's very particular way of speaking. What she uncovers are the various layers of oppression re-created by an oppressed mother and practised on her daughter through constant and simultaneous affirmation and denial of her right to exist. Exclusion, taboo, transgression and need for purification are expressed through food, clothing, gifts, memories and language. Above all language.

Almost every one of the short passages that make up this novel circles around a single turn of phrase, twisting it, examining all its possibilities. The book is a brilliant exposition of the destructive potential of language. Hyvrard plays with vocabulary and grammar, deconstructing the French language to reveal the minute psychological effects that are so deadly and so difficult to identify. As the reader may imagine, such an approach makes the work a translator's nightmare and ultimate challenge. My colleague, J.-P. Mentha, and I have tried to maintain the flavour and intent of every one of Hyvrard's sentences without the result becoming incoherent in English. When she invents new words we invent also; when she distorts grammar and habitual sentence structures we do likewise. Bumpy sentences in this text are not due to sloppy translation; they exist to make the reader look harder at language and think about its premises and possibilities. We have tried our utmost not to insinuate ourselves between the writer and her words. On occasion we have been reduced to explanatory footnotes but have kept these to a minimum, assuming that the reader prefers a subtle read to a discourse on language.

The dead girl in the lace dress is the mother's precious china doll in its coffin-like box. This doll is the model offered to the girl children – Annie in particular – and is the central metaphor of the book. Like her model, Annie is entombed in the family apartment (but is clearly unsatisfactory as a china doll), and she is struggling desperately to create a life she can call her own.

This is one of the most powerful evocations of a mother-daughter relationship that has gone to the bad that I have read. It is a crucial addition to the literature on women and available to women. Hyvrard herself interprets it also as an extended metaphor on 'cannibalisation', be that technological, as in the effect of television on viewers' perception; racial, as in the treatment of Jews by the Nazis; or economical, the sucking dry of the 'developing' countries by the 'developed' world. In this way she integrates this text into the political issues of the body of her work. Certainly the effort of the narrator to claim her right to her body, opinions and personhood is a major thread throughout Hyvrard's writing. For her, the female body is always a political body and her narrator's task is always to find a language that will not permit women's experience to be crushed or reabsorbed by the dominant discourse.

Jennifer Waelti-Walters
University of Victoria
June 1995

NOTES

1 *Les Prunes de Cythère,* 1975; *Mère la mort,* 1976; *La Meurtritude,* 1977; *Les Doigts du figuier,* 1977 – all published by Editions de Minuit, Paris; *Le Corps défunt de la comédie, traité d'économie politique,* 1982 (Le Seuil, Paris); *Le Silence et l'obscurité, réquiem littoral pour corps polonais,* 1982 (Montalba, Paris); *Auditions musicales certains soirs d'été,* 1984; *La Baisure* suivie de *Que se partagent encore les eaux,* 1985; *Canal de la Toussaint,* 1986; *Le Cercan,* 1987; *La Pensée corps,* 1989; *La Jeune morte en robe de dentelle,* 1990 – all published by Editions Des Femmes, Paris; *Ton nom de végétal,* forthcoming from Editions Trois, Montreal.

2 Translations into English of Hyvrard's works: *Mother Death* (*Mère la mort*), by Laurie Edson (University of Nebraska Press, 1988); 'Fingers of the Fig-tree' (*Les Doigts du figuier*), by Helen Frances as part of her MA thesis for Victoria University of Wellington, New Zealand; *Waterweed in the Wash-houses* (*La Meurtritude*), by Elsa Copeland (Edinburgh University Press, 1996).

3 Julia Kristeva, *Powers of Horror,* trans. Léon Roudiez (New York: Columbia University Press, 1982).

IN–DIFFE–RENCE. She carefully detaches each syllable, makes the 'FF' whistle like a whip, and gloats over each sound as she would over a candy she adores. In her mouth, pieces of words are like monsters. She beams like a thousand suns. She wants me to become like her, a member of the master species. But I disappoint her: I do have feelings.

Neither denial nor negation nor cancellation. There's not. Nullification.

There's not.* That's the phrase she throws at me, a shovelful of earth to seal a tomb or more precisely a grave, a tomb which would not be, since her relation to the world doesn't allow the use of the verb to be. She doesn't say 'You are my daughter', but 'I have three children'. She speaks like a forlorn little girl trying to remember what she can possibly be doing here in this place where there's not.

* 'There is' in French is rendered by the verb to have, *il y a*, hence the possibility that the mother can avoid the verb 'to be'. We can find no way of avoiding this contradiction as it occurs throughout the book. – Trans.

She asks me what I want to eat. Not to cook it for me but to explain to me that it isn't good.

I don't know what use I am to her.

Not a mother, she still has hers, hard-faced, hat pulled low over her eyes. Not a scapegoat, my father fills that role to perfection. I am rather that piece of dirt which absolutely must be eliminated for the world to be nice and clean.

I stay sitting on the stool.

She doesn't want me to climb on her knee. I'm too big. I can't remember a time when that was possible. I must have been born too big.

I often complain to her about the bad treatment inflicted on me by my brother. She invariably answers 'Be quiet. Otherwise he will take it out on me.' I can't tell whether she is talking about my father or her son.

The only element of discrimination is the word 'good.'

Good is what she wants me to eat. Not good what *I* would like to eat. Other people's food, their gifts, their shared meals, the school cafeteria where you can fool around. What can be bought outside and which leaves time for things other than nutrition.

Good has nothing to do with the actual taste of food. Neither hers nor mine. Only with the idea she has of what health is. The avoidance of any foreign contact. Can be called good, only what she decides, chooses and prepares. With her own hands. Is good only what comes from her.

Good or not good, the outside world could be ingested. But it is not good. None of it should be eaten. There is no outside. There's not.

Food should have no other taste than that of there's not.

No dressing, no oil, no cream, no salt, no sugar, no pepper which is so bad for one's health, no vinegar which attacks the stomach, no seasoning that you don't know what's in it, no butter or just a tiny bit.

As for herbs and spices, she'd never have that stuff in her kitchen! It's good for those who cook with smelly old grease.

We are 'nice people'. We eat without feeling anything.

There's no question of telling her one has had enough. That would imply that there could be some distance between her hand and our mouth, when in fact there is none.

She conscientiously force-feeds her monstrous cannibal brood.

She has three children.

She explains that one should not have friends 'because then one is led to go out'.

We girls have the job of drying the dishes. Never our brother, he's a boy. In spite of her nickname 'the slippery slow-worm' my sister goes along with it fairly cheerfully. Me, I'm always looking for a way to sneak off. I hesitate between two courses of action: getting permission to leave her to do the drying or shutting myself in the WC. The situation gets tense when we get to the saucepans. They may be aluminium, our mother being on the cutting edge of progress, but they're heavy and it's discouraging. Quickly soaked, the tea-towel doesn't dry any more. If we say so, it's worse: 'Tea-towels must be used sparingly!' I don't understand what that means since she won't let them be left to dry . . . I like the 'do-it-all' pot because of its name, and the prolonged thunk that the casserole pans and pots make on the stone of the sink. With my sister, I nick-named the pots and pans the artillery. No doubt because my father is teaching the laws of ballistics to my brother.

I would die if it weren't for my brother Pierre. He doesn't give in to the tortures my father inflicts on him. I learn that this is possible. He keeps repeating all the time 'Struggle for life', in English.

My older sister has taken pity on me. She thinks I wear the funniest get-ups. She teaches me how to tie scarves.

She also explains to me how to look for things in a dictionary. You don't turn the pages one by one but in bundles to get nearer. You refine afterwards, reading the words one by one.

She demands that my sister and I hang our panties on the line folded up. She shows us what to do so that their shape doesn't show. They must be folded in four with the gusset inside. Otherwise it isn't proper. We point out that that doesn't dry as quickly. She doesn't want to know.

When she questions me to find out whether I'm having my period, she points an accusing, avid and disgusted finger at my belly and asks 'That's running?' 'That', the stuff my belly is made of and also what is running out of it. It's the same. The shapeless dough she finds so hard to work into shape. Not for want of trying.

She tells the story that long ago a friend of ours, a nasty little girl, cut off one of our teddy bears' tongues. She can't recall if it was mine or my sister's. It doesn't matter. The main thing is that something should have been cut off. And if it is a tongue, so much the better.

Centre of everyone's attention, my sister blushes easily. I never do. My type of skin doesn't allow me to be shamed nor my humiliation to be seen. My mother regrets that. This quality bothers her, she is secretly chagrined but tries not to show it. I never get sunburnt or rather, if I do, I don't peel but tan beautifully. The world has not forsaken me.

My brother is grounded. It's the term they use to say punished. He must stay in the house, going out forbidden.

My sister and me too. We're not punished. We're girls.

When my father leaves the apartment, he says to me 'I leave your mother in your care.'

I do my best to be up to it.

My sister is the object of my adoration. She has everything I don't have: a watch, a bra and boyfriends. Better still she is secretly finishing the table-mat I am embroidering for Mother's Day. She works on it after lights out using a flashlight. I am not conscious of feeling gratitude towards her. In this house there are no words to describe feelings.

Just a drop! She tells my father who is offering her a drink. Holding out her glass, she gets ready to be extravagant, because one must now and then allow oneself some satisfaction. The body needs it. It gives a little lift! But not too much, because one must not set a bad example to the children.

Just a minute! The phrase 'Come here, just a minute!' is the equivalent of a summons to the police-station on business concerning you. Whereas 'Come over here a minute!' means I'm going to have a spot removed, 'Come here just a minute' indicates a choice between the letting out of a seam or the moving of buttons.

'Just a second!' is the time it will take to try something on, during which I will have to keep still so that she can see if it's all right. I must perform absurd and precise movements on command. Raise my arms, turn round, bend over. 'Don't wriggle like that,' she says as I squirm with impatience, irritation and a mute revolt against her power to make me hold grotesque positions imposed by necessities I don't understand.

She's going to do just a touch! . . . of ironing or of vacuuming. What else could it be? Certainly not just a touch of her fist. She always has a soft touch. It can't be just a touch of the gas pedal or the brake since my father doesn't want her to drive even though she has her licence. Just a touch is of ironing or vacuuming because it is so easy for her, who is a good housekeeper, and that's not the only thing she has to do, with all she has to do. With just a touch of the iron or the vacuum everything remains decent. No chance of taking forbidden pleasure in it.

Just a bit more. This expression recurs in the sentence 'Better to spend just a bit more!' She tries by this formula to teach me to recognise what I should choose. She wants me to give up my ordinary tastes. That's what she calls what I like. When she doesn't manage it, then they've palmed off any old thing on me.

She doesn't want anything to do with my presents. After a certain time she gives them back to me. She doesn't need them. She doesn't need anything. She's sacrificed herself for us. The only objects she accepts from me, when at last I have managed to make some space, are the empty jam-jars, cake-tins and empty fruit-dishes that I must give back to her when they have fulfilled the filling up. Thus filled, she can give them to me to give. She stuffs me in an endless noria. I've known the word since the trip to Spain. Gifts must come from her exclusively. Shoes she can't wear anymore but which are still good. Eau de cologne that she tells me not to waste because it costs a lot. Or clothes I need and which she will wash herself because if I did it I'd ruin them.

I'm a fraction of her three children. The weak part which crumbles, bridles and does not keep its shape. The one that smashes, breaks, dirties, is clumsy and careless, speaks badly and who, in a general sense, creates more work. She doesn't hold it against me. A mother understands everything.

She buys us dresses at the Galeries Lafayette. I see some I would like but she finds them ridiculous. We always choose what she wants. No means of doing otherwise. She knows what's necessary for me. I am like her, broad-hipped.

After doing the buying, we go and eat ice-creams in the basement. We walk through a department full of gleaming dishes set out on white tablecloths. She gives the order to avoid getting caught on anything. I discover fine china and crystal. There are services of 44, 56 or 74 pieces. I don't know what that corresponds to. I stay to look at the arabesques of leaves and birds. She tells me to come along. She gets impatient. I would like to stay a little bit longer.

In a corner of the basement there is a self-service. You walk in front of the servers who put the ice-cream in the dishes. You can choose your flavour. My sister has strange tastes, she likes lemon and pistachio. *I* prefer raspberry.

Mummy is allergic to strawberry. We eat them with big spoons which we find very amusing. I think it's funny to eat standing up. At home it's forbidden. She explains to me that it's so that people don't stay for hours. I find this idea peculiar. It's the best moment of the day. All three of us are happy.

As soon as we are home, she undertakes to put the finishing touches to the garment she has just bought me. Although I insist that it is fine as it is, she finds it absolutely necessary to add a fastener to the belt, to move the buttons or even to let out a seam. There is no way that I can ever wear it as it is. Whatever the size, it must be too small for me.

She always makes a third between my clothes and me.

There is some mummy, that gluey stuff that gets itself into everything I do.

'Zazou!' she says tugging at the bright little scarf I've tied round my neck.* I don't know what that means. But there is something threatening in her face. I'm frightened . . .

Things are divided into two categories: the 'it might come in useful' and the 'junk'. She alone can tell the difference. In the 'it might come in useful' are put above all the scraps of cloth, the wool and the clothing. Except the feathers and the lace. In the junk, all the rest. Especially what I have and which doesn't come from her, the dust-traps, the frills and furbelows and the little souvenirs brought back from trips. The 'it might come in useful' is packed in cardboard boxes tied up with string which she alone has access to. She has sovereign right over the opening and the use. It is imperative that the junk be thrown away. Books belong neither in the 'might come in useful' nor the junk. They are not.

Every time she's been rummaging, everything has to be put back together again.

A 'zazou' is a Teddy-girl or a zoot-suiter – Trans.

The name is used to identify the thing within a narrow concept, closed, itemised, and making codification possible. The matter she talks about has no name. She denies me the right to an existence of my own, desires, a will and a sphere of activity. What is mine is hers, my clothes, my belongings, my body.

The unnameable is not what has no name but rather what one is incapable of naming or, more simply still, what one doesn't want to name. What one doesn't call anything because one doesn't have a use for it.

I am 'that'. This matter she gave birth to and in which she does not see a person but something she has a duty to shape.

Out of this unpromising matter that she was supplied with she is carving her clone. Me. The part of me she uses to fill with herself.

Her personal universe consists in relating not to people but to matter. There are two kinds: Food and annie. There is a principal matter which is the focus of all her attention, food, and a secondary matter, less interesting, the annie. This matter is difficult to work, it is recalcitrant, it doesn't keep the shape it is given, it escapes. It isn't like food which you can choose as you wish.

Some annie. She is burdened down by this poor quality raw material, so difficult to work. It's not her fault. She wasn't allowed to choose. What she has managed to do isn't so bad, given such poor raw material.

That space where something happens about which I know nothing. Something happens in the place where she says 'There is nothing'. In the place about which she says 'there's not', there is something however: some annie.

Her obsession, to get rid of the world, as if it were gluey matter to be eliminated. As soon as she sees a possibility of going back to her organisation, she exploits it. Ant's work.

I can't remember a single consolation.

I am sitting on the kitchen stool. I mustn't touch anything or I would break everything. Except for the most fragile things, then I would be clumsy and careless.

I'm the rag-doll she plays mummy with. The other one mustn't be damaged, the real one, the china one. She's asleep in the large wooden box her father made.

We girls don't have the right to touch it. Only to look at it when, from time to time, our mother ceremoniously lifts the lid.

In the forest she teaches me the names of the flowers. The yellow jonquil and the blue periwinkle don't present any difficulty. They are so different in shape, size and colour that they can't be mistaken for each other. When we see some I say their names with all the joy in the world she gives me. We are happy and pleased with each other. I have the most beautiful mother on earth. She makes me pretty clothes and lovely bows on my checked smock. I also know the wood anemone, the first flower of spring and even the pasque flower. There are some where we picnic at Fontainebleau. I am very proud to know the lesser celandine. She taught me to recognise it by its bulbous root. I have discovered, all by myself, that it can often be found along the lanes. She tries in vain to teach me how to distinguish the true-love from the cinquefoil. She doesn't tell me anything about the common rock-rose, this miniature sunflower.

The verb 'to slip off' has several uses.

When I move away from her, I slip off.

She also uses it for men in general. She says that 'it's better to marry them because otherwise they slip off'.

As for its compound 'slip off on',* it is reserved for the goods I bring home. Especially food. I get just about anything slipped off on me.

When we set off on holidays my pockets are full of my personal supplies. I have been to Uniprix after school to buy them. It's forbidden but I go just the same. I got palmed off on me all I could buy with my pocket money. Candies, sweets, cakes. Those weeks I even give up the *Mickey Mouse Comic*.

They haven't managed to choose me a name for myself alone. They gave me the second name of my older sister. She never misses a chance of explaining to me: my name is hers too, but the opposite isn't true.

* We decided to keep the word play and take the risk of awkward English. Hyvrard uses the same verb on pp. 15 and 28, 'to palm off on'. – Trans.

I am part of her. A second growth.

My mother calls us by one name or the other without distinction.

I protest.

She thinks I make a lot of fuss over very little.

– Better to be a live ant than a dead lion!

That's what she tells me again and again when I complain to her about what they inflict on me. Push me into the nettles. Burn me with cigarettes. Steal my best stamps.

'Better to be a live ant than a dead lion!' That's what she explains to me when she agrees to discuss all that with me. Most of the time she merely seizes the opportunity to remind me:

– You should just stay here with me.

I'm a slob. There's no way to be close up against her body. She always keeps me at a distance so that I don't dirty her.

It doesn't keep her from constantly priding herself on the always exemplary role she plays for us, her three children: chiefly for me, the especially pampered littlest one.

I already know all about what separates her body and language, her flesh and her mouth, her womb and the world. Everything but the tragic name of the fault: beheading.

– You're getting water everywhere!

She doesn't shout. Only she has the tight harsh voice she uses when she is VERY DIS–PLEAS–ED. Stressing the R, she emphasises the very and then detaches the syllables. She is at the height of her anger.

– You're getting water everywhere!

I must have got out of the bath-tub, washed a glass or rinsed a sock. Once again it's she who will wipe it up, she has so much work already.

– You're getting water everywhere!

She goes and gets the floor-cloth. She doesn't want me to touch it, it's dirty. She has already told me, water, to be careful. I spill it everywhere. She sometimes lets me fill the carafe. But then I make it squirt.

– You can mess up your life in five minutes! . . .

She doesn't explain what it means 'to mess up your life' but it must be terrible because she threatens us girls with it whenever we want to go out into the street. In five minutes? She needs more than that to take a photograph. The time for a walk down the avenue, in a quarter of an hour, you already have the time to ruin it several times.

I know what messing up paper means. I am given some only if I show the used sheets. Messing with food, I know too. It's when I leave some on my plate while Chinese children have nothing to eat. I even know what 'messing up' plaster* means, as grandfather used to do. I am rather proud of knowing the expression. It's complicated, rare and fun. It proves me right. When I mess up it's not necessarily bad. Who knows, maybe I am building the wall that will separate me from her.

To mess up your life, what on earth can it mean since we are told we can improve ourselves everyday? 'Your life'

* JH uses *gâcher. Gâcher* is the correct word for mixing plaster (in English the term is mudding); in all other circumstances it means to spoil. This is our compromise – Trans.

what is it? Sometimes she talks about 'life' with her mother or her aunt. She says 'in life, you don't always do what you want' but 'your life' what's that? Life, it's outside, in the street, the place where she doesn't want us to go, us girls. But 'your life'? Outside belongs to everyone. How could there be an outside belonging to oneself. There is no 'your life'.

'You can mess up your life in five minutes.' The irreversibility is frightening, in so short a space of time. It must be something terrible such as murder which takes you straight to the gallows. It can happen in a fit of anger or panic, in five minutes, that's possible, and afterwards there's nothing you can do, you're guillotined. That's to mess up your life? But she says it about girls going out and they don't look mean. Beautiful rather. You wouldn't think of them as murderesses. They don't look like those terrible faces you see at the dentist's in the magazines my father doesn't want us to read.

Behind. If need be, you can say 'behind the hedge' when you go there. But you have to take care and hide and then put stones on the pieces of paper so they don't blow away. Once you have finished, nothing must show.

Behind. She can also undo a seam behind so it pulls less. Provided of course that the manufacturer has allowed enough width, which is not always the case.

– I'm going to put you on a diet.

At last, she sees the possibility of controlling everything that goes into me, of abolishing this freedom I have left to guzzle and destroy myself rather than submit.

– I'm going to put you on a diet, she says avidly.

Not 'you must' or 'you should go on a diet'. It's neither an order nor a piece of advice, but an administrative measure she takes.

She is thinking aloud. She talks about me as though I were not there. It's the 'you' that creates the uneasiness. One can't say you to someone who isn't there. The correct form would rather be 'I am going to put Annie on a diet'.

– I am going to put you on a diet.

She talks to me as she would to her doll. I am the substitute for an absence. An absence incarnate – a non-body.

The purpose isn't to make me lose weight, on the contrary she fattens me up, but to make sure that I don't ingest anything which would give me pleasure.

She institutes the body police.

Above all let's not celebrate holidays, they might link us to the world . . .

She wouldn't mind sending me shopping but I'll let them palm off any old thing. Not droopy lettuce, stringy green beans or sprouting potatoes but any old thing.

I can be in the world only in a fusional, fused, melted relationship. That's to say in not being there.

In my hands, the food the world gives is any old thing, that neutralised neutrality. She knows what's good. Lettuce with very little dressing, green beans with little butter and mashed potatoes just like that with nothing at all, because it is better still when there is no. Food, it's *her* business. She knows all about it. Not I. *She* chooses. Me, I get palmed off on.

There is no other verb if I buy anything. I can only be the passive object of the dishonest practices of a hostile outside world. Fortunately, she is here. She wouldn't mind sending me shopping but I'll let them palm off any old thing on me. Better she should go herself. The verb to shouldgo presents no danger.

When my father doesn't come home, we get bored.

When we begin to worry she invariably answers 'I'm waiting for my orders.'

She looks like a little girl lost who is afraid of punishment. She no longer seems invulnerable. A little bit more grown up, we could almost feel sorry for her.

But no, she doesn't need anything. She's sacrificed herself for us.

As soon as I cough, she is a much better mother. When I'm in bed, she applies a mustard poultice to my chest. I loathe this cold, gooey thing which makes the skin burn. She plonks a thick towel over it and forbids me to move. As time goes on it hurts more and more. In the end, I beg her to remove it. She cheerfully answers keep it a bit longer. Over the years she has improved her technique. There now exist mustard plasters which go all round the thorax. These are the ones she finds the best. She likes to care for me. She has always taken good care of us, her three children, it's her whole life.

I won't manage to get married, that's certain. Nobody will have me. They all agree on this.

I shall remain a spinster, the case is closed. That being so, I might as well get an education.

To do everything men do. Drink wine. Smoke in the street. And even grab the paper as soon as my father has put it down. Before my mother. Thus asserting my position in the family hierarchy.

Besides, she doesn't contest it. I am a tomboy. Tomboy or tom-girl?

– It'll pass for you!

If she said 'it will pass' you could understand it as an encouragement to get over the pain. But it would be better to use a near present as, while holding a sick person's hand, one would say 'Breathe in deeply and out slowly, it is going to pass!' 'It' would then represent the affliction that the verb to pass would allow one the hope that one would soon be rid of. 'Is going' would allow the waiting for the deliverance at the end of the sentence, joining the world of the living a bit as in the expression 'How's it going?' while 'to pass' would eliminate the waste.

'It will pass' in the future could if necessary refer to an era whose end the Elders, in the strength of their experience, would predict. In that case one would not say 'it's going to pass' because the world doesn't change fast enough for one to use a present, but 'it will pass' meaning 'it is going to pass' on a historic scale. One would encourage an upset body politic to hold fast. But it can't be that, since the war has ended. She didn't say 'it's going to pass' to help me fight the pain, nor 'it will pass' to pass on the memory. She said:

– It'll pass for you!

There certainly is a future there, but it applies only to me. It's not a collective future, but a personal fate. Something, it, will leave me. A volatile and ephemeral substance which will not take on me. A bit like blueing makes washing whiter. The blue put in the water does not stay on the cloth. If you take it out of the tub, it will pass out of it. Certain of her housekeeping qualities, she is unconcerned. The colour is of no importance. Nothing marks. Nothing stains. With scarlet water or tap water, she overcomes everything. She's fearless. With a loud and cheerful laugh:

– It'll pass for you.

I just confessed my love for the seventh-floor neighbour, a shy young man with an angora sweater: Michel Lafererre.

This cellular thing which has no compassion for the pain exploding everywhere around her. The wailing of my grandmother whose son hasn't come back. The cousins' perfidious innuendoes. Accounts settled through the children. References to the black market, in a wheelbarrow or on a bike. Development of the trials reported on the radio. The weeklies all filled with pictures of the horrors. She is absolutely unmoved. All of this doesn't concern her. She has three children. She goes 'pffftt' through her lips. It's really not very important. I have truly uninteresting preoccupations.

– With a little girdle, you'd be better!

Her voice takes on a tone of complicity. We are between women. She is trying to convince me. But I don't see how I could climb trees in that. There is between the girdle and the world what my mathematician of a father calls an incompatibility. She knows it too. She returns often to the attack.

– With a little girdle, you'd be better!

She shows me hers, takes out the bones, those stiff white rods over which she reigns and reassures me: 'Not one as big of course, but a small one, supple, providing a light support . . .' To soften the thing, she mobilises all the resources of her vocabulary. Small, supple, light. She is trying to seduce me, I am wary.

– With a little girdle, you'd be better!

I wear the panties she buys me, the vests she buys me, the cardigans she knits for me, the pretty dresses she buys me and the skirts in the material she has chosen that I sew under her supervision. But for the girdle she needs my consent. She must convince me. She takes the time to explain to me. We pretend to get on well together.

– With a little girdle, you'd be better!

'It makes for a slim waist under dresses.' She rolls her eyes, as in the silent films. She's going to buy my agreement. Of course there is in her sentence an 'it' that worries me, but is it really the same as in 'it pulls there' that she utters when she fingers my skirt? Waist? Slim? Dress? And if she were right, if with it I'd be better? She notices my hesitation and puts on an enigmatic air. She is getting ready to initiate me into the secrets of accomplished women.

– With a little girdle, you'd be better!

What does it mean, better? Prettier? The adjective doesn't apply to the body.

Back from a party, when she wants to pay herself a compliment, including us, the girls, in her satisfaction, she says 'we weren't the worst'. Pretty can refer only to what one should wear to find a husband . . . 'You'd be better . . .' is it the superlative of to be all right? But this notion is not accepted. The word itself is unknown. 'That's done' or 'that's not done', 'it's nice' or 'it's not nice', but all right? As for pleasure, it only exists in the phrase 'Do it to please me', and is heavily threatening. Good is definitely unusable because it is reserved for what she has decided to make me eat. In any case, the superlative would be better.*

– With a little girdle, you'd be better.

The sentence is equivocal. Does she mean more comfortable as subject or more presentable as object? The verb 'to wouldbe' coalesces on both sides of the rubber. It's no longer a girdle, it's glue.

To find the words to tell the horror she inspires in me. This constant attempt to remove me from the world.

Whenever there is question of something other than

* The adverbial and adjectival forms are different in French: *mieux* and *meilleur*. – Trans.

herself, she answers with the unique expression 'there's not'.

I must not touch anything. I am a caged bird on the stool in her kitchen.

Smugly she recounts how one day one of us threw her bottle on the floor and never accepted it again.

She doesn't remember which one.

It doesn't matter. The main thing is that there be one of the two who doesn't drink milk any more. So there is a break at last.

It's through this fault that *she* breathes.

My brother never stops getting himself into trouble. This time he has opened the sluices of the lake and flooded the countryside. My father, furious, beats him black and blue and drags him naked through the water and the rock garden. I can hear yelling, moaning and cries for help. My mother doesn't move. I am dumbfounded.

She explains adoption to me. The difference between a mother and a mummy. A mother is a woman who looks after a child, but, even very good, she isn't a mummy. A mummy is the one we are born from and who is able to understand everything. Adopted children don't have their mummy. *I* am lucky, I have one.

I haven't understood the difference between a mother and a mummy very well. Her distinction hasn't convinced me. The mummy isn't what she says. I would say, rather, that a mummy is a woman who looks after a child. A mother is the one in whose belly you've been. I can't have been in her belly since she doesn't have one. She must have adopted me. She's my mummy and I must have a mother somewhere else.

She's going to put me in the hands of a doctoress. It sounds like mistress but it's much rarer. I have never seen one. I haven't understood whether it was because I have swollen glands, I'm too fat or do not obey her.

'Put in the hands' what does it mean? There is a hired hand, give a hand, hand gun . . . But in the hands? It's to deposit a thing somewhere. She is going to put me in the hands of a doctoress who will take things in hand. The me-thing-in-hand.

Indeed one says 'in the arms', but it's in the movies in *Notorious*, Ingrid Bergman and Cary Grant.

She's going to put me in the hands of a doctoress who will take the thing in hand. It's because I don't obey. Eat as I might, I don't lose weight. It's because of my glands.

She's going to transfer me from one container to another. Being very careful not to tip me over.

She has three children. The verb to have is reserved for her. She carries with her everywhere the proof of her existence, the family record book in which we are all three inscribed.

Whenever it's a question of me the negative form is inevitable. My thoughts, my wishes, my feelings, she cancels them out with a 'there's not'. She does not know the verb 'to be'. She does not know how to say 'I am', but only 'I have three children'. She cannot say 'Annie is' or better still 'you are'. She could say 'you don't have' or 'Annie doesn't have', but that would call for an object. She doesn't see what I might be able to not have for that would imply thinking about it.

She would gladly reassemble this void in an impersonal phrase such as 'Annie doesn't have of it' or 'you don't have', but she would not be reassured for all that. This name or this first name would still call to mind something which would keep drifting around looking for an object. It would put her in the shade.

That's why she closes the last gate. That empty person is not a person. At most a piece of ground that comes under her jurisdiction. A named ground. A no-grounds.

To have no grounds for. There's not.

To speak her language at last. To dare to tell her 'You don't have'.

Back from the holidays, we must unload the caravan parked in front of the building. We start a noria. We carry blankets, bags and clothes. We must also take back into the flat what she doesn't have another of, such as the pressure cooker. She wraps it in an old pair of my father's underpants, and gives it to us to carry.

My sister and I, we refuse.

Science is her idol, the major element of her system. Whenever she invokes it, there is nothing more to be said. She teaches me the parts which reinforce her order, the instinct of self-preservation to justify the exactions, the hierarchy to subject me to her will and the psychology to reject the ideas which are in my head.

She crushes the whole of human knowledge, conscientiously, in order to extract from each discipline what is going to enslave me. She takes my education to heart, perverting all that could reach me from the outside.

She does not mediate the whole world, she uses it to bind me to her. She never stops carving out of the quick what she is going to be able to suck. It's what she calls her trust in life.

Then she has the same greedy and satisfied look as when she is sucking the marrow out of the bone in the beef stew.

She always comes between the world and me. I must receive nothing from it, nor give it anything. There must not be any exchange.

She settles into me like a necrophagous insect feeding on my putrefaction. I must not be, so that a hand could not be put between her and me. She assimilates me to herself. She makes me her. She mehers. She loves me.

If there really is no Annie, how is it that she is so good at preventing me from growing?

Predatoriness. The other's living kept in the earth's magma. Humification. Humiditation. Humiliation. To keep the other's living in the world of earth. To annihilate. To annul. To nullate. To keep the other's living indistinguishable from the earth.

She makes a fusionist out of me. A plant assigned a forced residence on her territory.

She cultivates me in a pot.

I can't free myself of my fascination for the mistletoe smothering the apple-tree in the meadow. I don't know the word parasite.

The mistletoe loves the apple-tree.

There is some mummy, that gluey stuff which interferes in everything I do. It forces me to return the books I have been given, tears the pages out of the one I'm reading and demands to see what I write.

There is some mummy everywhere.

I am trying on a new garment. She is close beside me to see if it's all right.

– It pulls here!

She has grabbed the cloth of my skirt between her thumb and forefinger and pulls to show just where it pulls. On my buttocks of course.

– It pulls here!

She smoothes the fabric over my body to show clearly that, in fact, it pulls of course, on my buttocks, in fact. Try as she may to let out the seams and move the buttons, pulling the cloth tight on my behind, it still shows. The proof:

– It pulls here!

Here, it's the spot where it pulls, where she pulls to show that it pulls, since it's where it pulls here. Here, my buttocks. Here, her hand. Here, the meeting place of her hand and my posterior.

– It pulls here!

'It's here that it pulls' would be clearer. 'Here' would then be the place where it would happen.

– It pulls here!

She could just as well say 'here, it pulls' or 'here, pull it' or 'pull here, it' or 'pull it here' or 'it, here, pull'. All these sentences would be similar. For her, language is not used to express ideas but to camouflage them. It and here are interchangeable. The sentence is polar:

– It pulls here!

It, doesn't cover only the mush of the ideas which she has pulverised, it, it's also, it, pull here, my buttocks and her hand indiscriminately. It, it's the place where it . . .

– It pulls here!

It, my buttocks, my skirt, her hand and what she has made of my thought. How is it that I do not die?

– But you're big now! . . .

That's usually when she wants something from me that she can't impose otherwise. Most of the time, that I agree like a good girl to stay at my grandparents' or that I give up all thought of being cuddled . . .

But, when it's a matter of staying at home while she takes my brother to see Gérard Philipe in *Le Cid* at the theatre then I am 'too little'.

I suffer simultaneously from the inconveniences of being big and being little, without ever enjoying the advantages of the one or the other.

In a secret corner of my brain, that she has no access to, I practise figuring out the rate of deathness.

For this peculiar thing, there is no word.

To defecate is unknown.

To shit is out of the question in so distinguished a home. My father uses it sometimes. Then there's a scene.

To do is reserved for what she has to do, and she has a lot to do, the more so in that she has much more than that to do.

What's left then is the simple to have a poo. We had a poo when we were little. But since then, we have stopped. We are big.

Especially me, whom she refuses to let climb onto her knee.

I have already read all the books in the bookcase, including Edmund Rostand's *L'Aiglon,* and *Cyrano de Bergerac* which I like even better. I know La Fontaine's *Fables* by heart.

My sister has even lent me her school prize, *Nils Holgersson's Marvellous Journal.* Gilt-edged, I have the right to touch it only after washing my hands. In it you can see a little boy crossing the sky on the back of a gander. It's the most beautiful of all the books there are here.

I read on the sly those my father has forbidden, *Marion Delorme* and *Cinq-Mars.* When I hear him coming, I put them under the bed . . . My sister doesn't dare. I feel a bit scornful of her. My father often says that of the two I am the elder . . .

It seems there are others in the basement, but we aren't allowed to read them because there is no room and because we are too little, we girls, especially my sister who was born before me.

As I have already read everything, I buy shilling paperbacks. I can choose what I want. And that makes it possible to go down into the street and walk across the square. This is authorised. We do nothing bad. We go and buy a book.

– If I hadn't had three children . . .

It's the theme, the leitmotif, the obsession. We can't tell exactly what she would have done. We think we understand that she would have left him, but then we can't see why she always speaks well of him: 'He doesn't drink, he doesn't run around, he doesn't smoke.' We don't know what she would have done exactly. We just have the impression that we shouldn't be here. Especially me. 'Three children, it's too much', she tells me, me, the last one.

'If I hadn't had three children . . .'

Part of the negation is missing.* She ought to say 'If I had not had three children', but the block 'I had' cannot be split and even less so by a negation. 'Not' can frame the verb 'to have' only when referring to Annie. 'Not' cannot

* The negative is in two parts in French, *ne-pas*, and these surround the verb: *Si je n'avais pas eu trois enfants* would be the correct form; she uses *Si j'avais pas . . . .* Because English has a one-word negative, we have had to compromise – Trans.

follow a personal pronoun without invalidating it. 'I' can exist only when bolted to 'to have' and to its global complement 'three children'.

The negation could be 'If I have three children had not been', but this form cannot exist because she ignores the verb 'to be'. She would have to say 'If I have three children had not had'. But what on earth could be had or not had since to have cannot exist without its complement 'three children'? Thus the sentence becomes 'if I have three children had not had three children' and all these children indeed, that would be too much. So, she prefers to simply say:

– If I hadn't had three children . . .

– You who are intelligent! . . .

Her eyes gleam. I can see her forked tongue showing between her lips. She is pleased with herself. She has the good idea of flattering me to get what she wants: my silence.

– You who are intelligent! . . . Leave him alone! . . . That doesn't matter! . . .

She leans on me with all her weight, to model me on

her. I am intelligent to accept, without rebelling, the tortures and the despoliations imposed upon me by my brother, her beloved son. Intelligence, it's abdication, resignation, submission. You who are intelligent, do then as I do, don't struggle. I feel in my rachidian bulb the long needle she turns in it to destroy me. I do not cry out, I am intelligent. Eyes wide open, without weakening, I get accustomed to the horror of the world.

I am washing my hands, standing against the sink. She is sitting behind me on the stool. I have a pretty dress of bouclé wool. I feel her hands coming down on my hips and slowly descending over my buttocks.

One April morning, uplifted by spring, I walk into the kitchen. She smiles at me and says:

– You look like a Botticelli! . . .

My procreatress has looked at me, and I have found favour in her eyes. In heaven a thousand seraphim start to sing the Alleluia!

She lovingly polishes my buttocks, beaming at being such a skilful housekeeper. To be able to look after this piece of furniture of doubtful quality so well gives her a positive image of herself. So, abruptly, she feels like doing better: totally managing to chase away the bits of fluff which hang around under my skull. When I tell her about my suspicions she says:

– Oh that, that's just ideas in your head . . .

– You'll get married, you'll be happy, you'll have children!

What does she know about it? Why does she repeat that all the time?

– You'll get married, you'll be happy, you'll have children!

I don't see how. They say I'm a tomboy and no man will want anything to do with me . . .

– You'll get married; you'll be happy, you'll have children!

I don't see how. She accuses men of being the cause of all ill.

– You'll get married, you'll be happy, you'll have children!

I don't see how. Nothing must come out of my belly, especially not living flesh, because three children, it's too much!

– You'll get married, you'll be happy, you'll have children!

Why does she repeat this to me all day long? If it's a piece of advice, she should say 'Get married, be happy, have children'. And if it's an order, no need to speak of happiness. It must rather be a plan. She thinks aloud. The correct wording would be: 'I shall marry you off and you will have grandchildren for me!'

I don't see what the 'you' has to do with anything. Besides, when she uses it, it's quite a bad sign: 'You get water everywhere', or worse: 'You can't remember': generally speaking, the sentences she begins with this pronoun mean 'You should not be alive'.

So why does she say:

– You'll get married, you'll be happy, you'll have children!

Does she mean 'You'll shovel as much shit as I have'?

– Rabbits never stop producing brats!

That's what she calls women in gaudy colours, with long hair and baggy clothes. They produce brats. Matter that isn't unconnected to the diarrhoea you get when you eat green fruit. She, herself, has three children. We are not of the same verb as they are. *We* were not born. She has always had us. She will always have us. We are of another species.

My grandmother doesn't like me. My mother's mother is sorry that with this turned-up nose I look so much like my father. I am his spitting image. When I go to her house, she tries, while there is still time, to correct this error of nature, this vulgar protuberance, this organ of lèse-majesté. She pulls it sharply downward, massages it and tries to lengthen it. Maybe she is going to succeed. I have indeed seen in the middle of death's heads, that at the place in question, there is no bone.

– You cannot remember!

She doesn't say 'Do you remember?' or 'Don't you remember?' or better still: 'Don't you remember it?' or even poetically 'Do you have a remembrance of it?' No, whatever the event she refers to she maintains:

– You cannot remember!

She doesn't say 'You mustn't remember' because at a pinch this injunction could, with a little effort, seem like generosity towards the weakling I am. You could imagine her being told that to keep her from suffering . . . But it's not that.

– You cannot remember!

A ghost can't remember. *She* can. She alone can know what really happened. She alone can say what this shadow deprived of memory is.

– You cannot remember!

She doesn't say 'Annie doesn't manage to remember' because if there were a third person to whom she could speak of me, she would speak of her son.

– You cannot remember!

She doesn't say 'Annie has a poor memory' because by reciting the names of all the villages from Paris to Fontainebleau in the right order, I could show that that's not true. And even if it were, with practice I could improve.

– You cannot remember!

It's not 'Annie has a poor memory' but 'Annie cannot have any memory!' because Annie is not of the species endowed with memory. Annie is not of the same species as us. Annie isn't of the human species.

– You cannot remember!

The taboo pronoun can be uttered only with a negative. There can only be question of me as being unable to be. The negativity is consubstantial with me. The ideal of the sentence is: 'Annie doesn't have.'

– You cannot remember!

She doesn't say 'Annie does not remember her past' because the negative form would not be sufficient to reassure her. There is, between the idea of Annie and that of the past, an incompatibility.

– You cannot remember!

It's not only that Annie doesn't have a past, because in the long run, with time, she might perhaps end up having one. It's rather that the very idea of the past cannot apply to Annie.

– You cannot remember!

Annie is, she does know that. With all the work she makes. She is, indeed. But in an 'isity' which is as never having been. Annie has no future other than this present without a past. An eternity.

– You cannot remember!

And what would it mean if, on the contrary, she said 'You can remember!' Or even 'Surely you can remember!' or still 'You must remember!'? What would that mean? That she authorises me to remember? What? Having been little? No longer being little? Having grown? Having to grow? Leaving her one day to get married?

– You cannot remember!

She hasn't managed to invent the pronoun she needs 'You-not', the language which is not used for speaking but to prevent speaking. The code which occupies and cancels the space of difference. The pronoun of totalnity.

– You cannot remember!

What? That the apartment has a door?

The only link she has with the world is contempt. She tries to teach it to me. She doesn't manage. We get on less and less.

She looks through the glass wall at the object of her love. She lovingly lifts the lid. A light steam escapes from the pot. Bubbles rise and burst on the surface. She cranes her neck to observe the quivering of the meat more closely. In her right hand she holds a wooden spoon, the badge of her command. She plunges it into the stew which she stirs. She turns the pieces over and over. She is engrossed in her contemplation. With her left hand, she turns down the gas and says:

– It's going to cook nicely!

I constantly have the feeling that she wants to get rid of me. I make desperate efforts to please her. I live only the absolute minimum with the idea that she will make up her mind to keep me.

At least when I am with her.

The rest of the time I roam through woods and streams. I escape her. She feels it. Try as I may to play dead, she smells from the odour of my blood that something in me is still alive. A concavity which never stops attesting that it forms one half of the world. A cave which rejects the idea that history stops with it. A womb which hasn't given up giving birth.

I constantly have the feeling that she wants to get rid of me. I make desperate efforts to please her. I live only the absolute minimum with the idea that she will make up her mind to keep me anyway.

And yet when I am with her I always murmur the same word of distress.

She finally hears it. One day doubt comes to her and she wonders:

– Still, it *is* funny that you repeat that all the time . . .

Maybe everything isn't lost.

The wild hope that writing can, all by itself, prevent murder.

I am her glowing little doll whose arm she pulls off now and then to persuade herself that it's not happening to her.

I am very lucky to have a mummy who has sacrificed herself for us, her three children. Not all children have that. Some have been adopted. They have only a mother who looks after them, but they don't have a mummy. *I* am very lucky. When you are so lucky it's normal to stay beside your mummy. Whatever your age, whatever you have to do. Above all whatever little pile of ashes she makes you into: it's normal, she has sacrificed herself for you! I would be very ungrateful to want to live for myself, after all she's done for us.

She's happy for me to have children because she has had much satisfaction from us, her three children, but not too many because three children, it's too much. Little ones are sweet, when they're little.

She has just put a delicious slice of leg of lamb on my plate. I contemplate the pink and pearly flesh. I love it and get ready to savour it. I commune with myself a moment before the accomplishment of the rite. In my mouth there is the rich water of reverence.

Sure of herself, I would say arrogant if I knew the word, she holds the last slice on the dish with the tip of her fork. She lets it drip vertically over my food. The lamb is drenched with crimson blood.

She knows I loathe it. In sacrifice, she has an ease that astounds me. Incredulous, I look at my mother's hand above my fate. I see the juice of the dead and the living flowing.

Full of rage, I say to her:

– Why are you putting blood! You *know* I don't want any! She knows perfectly well. That's why she puts it on. Because it's good.

I'd run away if I could.

One day I shall run away.

She enjoys taking our photograph. She even enjoys it a lot. Especially the three of us together, us her three children. She makes us gather at the spot she has chosen and we must no longer move, really not at all. Arms at our sides. Usually right in the sun, and at noon, because of the light.

She has a huge camera we don't have the right to touch. When she wants to operate it, she pulls out the black bellows which she holds horizontally in front of her. Us, we wait. She bends over the object and looks into the viewfinder. She frames us. It lasts several minutes. It's not a simple operation. She has to gauge the effect. It won't do.

She makes us move forward. Backward. It still won't do. She wants us to change places, reverse places, get closer together. To draw apart is out of the question. It's still not right. She tries different arrangements to see which she would like best. We begin to wriggle. She calls us to order.

She arranges us like flowers in a vase. She always has problems because of our different sizes. Pierre is the tallest. Annie the shortest. It's Françoise who causes the least problem. She doesn't move and always does what she's told. My father is right. Of the two, *I* am the elder.

This time she's got it. It's me, the smallest one who should be put in the middle. We change places, looking sideways at each other, I would like the other two to hold me, but she doesn't want that. All she wants is that we be packed against one another. In one order and in another.

She would prefer Pierre to be on the other side. We begin to make fun of her. We change places. We get impatient because of the sun. We tell her to hurry. She explains that it's complicated, photography.

To see the picture clearly, she shades the viewfinder of her camera with her hand. She forbids us to protect our heads. She wants us to be seen clearly. Especially me who was so sweet when I was little.

It goes on and on. We melt into a compact mass, on the spot she has chosen. Bent over her Kodak-Pathé, she is totally into her intense pleasure. A few minutes more and she is going to press the shutter release.

My brother and my sister, I do remember.

My sister and I are in our room. We are doing our homework on the folding table. It's one metre square. My older sister's enormous Latin dictionary takes up all the room. I don't think it's fair that it should overflow on to my exercise books. I ask her to push over a little this Gaffiot that bothers me.

I can't bear this big dead-language dictionary.

She explains to me that life is worth living.

That she has had much satisfaction from us, her three children.

I am beginning to hate life.

I make a lot of work for her.

She must constantly fill the distance I try to create between us. She cancels it out with a perpetual 'You cannot remember' and annihilates me with a 'You'll get married, you'll be happy, you'll have children'.

She must also tug at my skirt all the time so that I won't imagine that, covering my belly and my buttocks, it belongs to me. She doesn't miss an opportunity to remind me that it pulls here, because I am broad here, as she is.

She can't bear there to be space between her and me. She stretches full out in my digestive tube. She is at home there, from the kitchen of my mouth to the WC of my anus. She does the housework there, seeing to it that there be neither salt, nor sugar, nor butter, nor sauce, nor cream, nor anything that could introduce some difference between the nutrients she has prepared for me and the food I have ingested.

In my digestive tube there is nothing but her duster with which she rubs my mucous membranes raw to the point of rendering them completely numb. I don't even bleed, I lose only words when my sphincters relax.

She has no idea about possessive adjectives. For clothes, she doesn't see the need for them. They fall indifferently under it, that and here, like the body. She doesn't say 'Your skirt pulls on your buttocks,' but 'It pulls here'. Besides it's not 'my' skirt but hers, and they are our buttocks.

As for my best clothes, she will never say 'your' red dress. It's true that there can be no confusion because such a strong colour, for a lady like her, it's not done.

Neither does she need to say 'your' shoes, since she is the one who polishes them. I do it too badly. Not to mention that on top of everything else my feet turn and what I need are arch supports to keep them straight.

The possessive adjective can't apply to my bed either, even though my father fights against her making them for us, the girls. The most he manages to obtain is that they should be 'the' beds, and not 'her' beds.

She only really knows how to use the possessive adjective to erase the presence of the one who shares 'her' room with her. She then uses grammar like a flame-thrower to clear a space around herself.

'Take it to my room' means that this object must be put away. There, I'm sure I won't ever have the right to touch it again. 'My' means a one-way ticket. It disappears into an abyss where everything melts.

'My' food, what's that?

This poo-ey mush she makes of the language. Her pretension of making me ingest it. This permanent confusion she creates between my mouth and my anus. This unique cloaca whose administration is hers. She is in her element. She has a lot to do. She doesn't have only that to do. She has three children. She is a good mother.

This fall into what she doesn't want to remember. This forbidden passage which gives her a glazed stare. This consummated sacrifice which makes her say 'There is not'.

She uses me to erect a barrier between her memory and herself, her desire and herself, between her anguish and herself. I am not her child. I am the site of the pain whose trace she has lost.

To finish the work begun. To give shape to the word that cannot be uttered. To let the void take over this space she believes to be hers. To die of languor. To die of consumption. To die of love. Not to accept anything from her any more.

To stop eating to relinquish completely to her this being which divides us. This bit of a corpse over which I still fight with her by my use of grammar.

To provide her with the place where there is no ground. The place where there is nothing. The place which is nothing. The no-grounds. The appeasement. That she might find peace at last in the empty vessel of my body. In the non-content of my digestive coffin. That she make herself a shelter from this wooden box.

To give her satisfaction, to make the space she has taken over into the empty space she seeks. The place for the memories she doesn't want to remember. To provide her with this empty place where nothing circulates. Neither the shit, nor the food. Neither the past nor the future. Neither the memory nor the word, nor the grammar, nor the song, nor the flesh of the world, nor the sap of the trees, nor the mystery of the living.

To relinquish this being to her completely. To let her lose herself in this flesh she thinks hers. To make of it a place where she will always lose herself. An organic bubble filled with the world. A moat filled with waterlilies and tritons. An insuperable rampart of water.

To die of hostility.

To keep for myself alone the absolute happiness of being alive. The suave voices of the seraphim. The place where I wait for her to come and fetch me from my crib and take me in her arms.

There is no mummy.

She has bought herself a suit 'to make herself more beautiful'. She can't manage to conjugate the verb to be. Fortunately there are two synonyms: to have and to make.

I can't manage to swallow my mother tongue. It's too digestive for me. I still prefer mathematics. There, at least, one knows where the zero is.

'Let no one enter here who is not a geometer.'

– I thought you'd never get to four!

It's the leitmotiv, she almost says it with tenderness, surprised that I should still be here, so grown up already. For once she talks of herself. She ingenuously admits her error. Evidently she made a mistake. It's rare enough for her to be able to do it without shame. It might even be the only slip in this exemplary life.

– I thought you'd never get to four!

There is no danger in having thought something since, fortunately, it's false. She is reassured now, the world remains carefully closed, no idea has cut into it. It was only an idea in the head, come from who knows where, and now flown away.

– I thought you'd never get to four!

Not 'that you'd never be grown up' because even in the negative conditional, the verb to be is too dangerous, except when the idea is to shape me in her image, as in the phrase 'With a little girdle, you'd be better'. Otherwise I must remain within the verb to have since she has three children, with its corollary applied to the rest of the world: 'There's not'.

– I thought you'd never get to four!

I came close to never being four years old. I made it just the same. But 'never' is here to cancel out my four years. Never mind the number of my years, with the word 'never' she need not worry. I'm certainly over four years old but I would never really have had them. Between the two, the adverb which cancels the getting and the verb to Ithought which is always conjugated in a tense of uncertainty. Between my age and myself always her belief in the never of my to wouldbe. An idea she has cultivated in her head in order to graft it in mine. There's no smoke without fire.

– I thought you'd never get to four!

So that's why she has not smothered me. She thought that of myself I would not live. She has been unable to thought [*sic*] that I would manage to grow up. Which goes to show that even she can be mistaken.

– You were so sweet when you were little! says she with regret.

She would have liked to keep me in a jar on a shelf.

She has always known how to turn the page.

Very pleased with herself she reveals to me the secret of her strength. She doesn't understand why I always ask her the same questions. She has already answered them. One didn't know. One couldn't know. One could not do anything and what could one do? What could one have done? Yes he died. No she cannot say how. Like that . . . Of exhaustion on the side of a road. She doesn't know exactly. She doesn't understand my attitude. What could one have done? What do I want her to explain? TO TUR–N THE PA–GE. She begins to detach the syllables, to chop the sentence finely. I am frightened.

– Come over here a bit!

Here is pointless, since I am beside her and must stay there. She ought to say 'Let's go over there', but the plural would let one suppose that we might do something together. These two verbs are reserved for her. She has three children. She has a lot to do. I can only come, but certainly not go. This verb would make it possible to leave the apartment.

– Come over here a bit!

She has discovered a spot on my garment. She must remove it immediately. Here in this case means indiscriminately the kitchen, the bathroom, the window where one can see better or the middle of the room to have more elbow room. At any rate a place where, not being there, she goes, because *she* has the right to go. Even the duty. She has a lot to do. Here means not there where she is, I beside her, but the unforeseeable place where I must follow her.

– Come over here a bit!

That means 'Let's go there'. In the apartment here is everywhere, not because it's too small to be divided between here and there but because it's her kingdom in which I have no place to hide and escape from her, except perhaps in the WC, the bolt protecting me from her. Here is where she is, whichever the room, including the son's or the daughters' rooms. There is no difference between here and there except when she fingers my skirt saying 'It pulls here!'. Here in this case refers to my buttocks, the only thing in the house which escapes from her even though she forbids the use of the verb to shit.

– Come over here a bit!

She has discovered a spot on my garment. The 'a bit' doesn't allow for any illusions concerning the fate awaiting me. In a normal state, there is nothing, if there is something, it must be destroyed. The correct expression would be 'Come here a bit and see if I'm over there'* but this crudeness has no currency in her house. She forbids my father to use slang in front of us. Moreover 'seeing' cannot apply to me. 'Doing' is already impossible for me, but could happen if need be, when unfortunately I upset, break or am clumsy and careless. Seeing is not possible, it would require feeling. Except in the expression 'Don't you see I'm busy?' which means 'Go away!' As for 'if I'm there', the implied doubt is unnecessary, she's always there. Thus she does not need to say 'Come here a bit and see if I'm over there', to threaten, it's enough for her to say:

– Come over here a bit!

* 'Viens voir un peu si j'y suis' is an expression similar to 'Get lost' or 'Clear off' – Trans.

She has discovered a spot on my garment. Where on earth have I been again to get that? I must have touched something, but what? She scrutinises the fabric, sizes up the enemy, defies it. That doesn't come from the kitchen, she does not let me approach the stoves. That could come from the bathroom but that doesn't look like it, and everything there is locked up behind white doors. Where on earth have I been hanging about? For outside there is never another verb. Would that be tar picked up on the way back from school? That must be it. I lower my head. Fortunately she has the Scarlet Water.

– Come over here a bit!

She's going to remove the spot. She always manages. She never leaves a ring. She doesn't discolour fabrics. She is perfect. We feel not gratitude, which might terrify her by a damp and oozing generosity, but gratefulness which brings us back to her belly. She has three children, but fortunately, she also has the Scarlet Water, the liquid colourless spot-remover in its glass flask, the essence which washes off the tar, traces of men, their sweat, their smell, their unambiguous talk, their filthy language. She opens the cupboard and pulls out the bottle, the cotton rag tied around the red stopper. In a circle, the label announces 'Scarlet Water' and, in smaller characters 'Dry Cleaning'. I look at this liquid which is not water and above all not the colour scarlet. The proof of the liquefaction of her grammar. I can't tear myself away from this contemplation.

– Come over here a bit!

She doesn't make me take off the garment, I could take advantage of that to slip away . . . It's the word used when I go away from her. She pours a bit of liquid on the white cloth. With emotion I breathe in the odour of mummy, that sublime vapour. She puts a threatening hand between the fabric and me and begins rubbing energetically starting from the outer edge. I am nearly in her arms. I feel the jolts of her love. I can't hold out against her ultimate weapon. This chemical which removes spots, marks and traces. I sniff deep into my lungs the evaporation of writing. I get used to perversion, negation, travesty. She subjects me to disappearance.

We are in the mountains. It is beginning to get cold. They are both going to sleep in the tent and the three of us in the car.

She has installed her camp-stove in the grass. She has cooked the vermicelli in the soup. We are sitting around her.

She fills our proferred plates. It's warm and good. She is gay. We are happy.

– Mountain pasture soup! she says, naming what makes me blossom.

I am proud to have such a beautiful mummy, so clever and so witty. I am invulnerable.

– Hurry up, that's not the only thing I've got to do.

That, is the work which consists in that. It could be said that it consists in feeding me, but it would not be that exactly. It would be better to say which consists in heaveeding me or in stuffeeding me. Both are suitable.

She does not want me to have been born. It would be better if I weren't here, but since I am here she might just as well stuffeed me. Her children, it's her whole life!

– Hurry up and swallow, that's not the only thing I've got to do!

That, is filling the container which she has hermetically sealed at one end, for fear that the precious matter should escape, which would render this filling up useless.

She has sewn up my anus so that nothing should be lost of what she has to get into me as fast as possible because that's not the only thing she's got to do.

In the mucus-membrane, she could have made openings, ladderwork or Venetian-style openwork, even a buttonhole with piping. But no. She hasn't put any button or hook, or snap fastener, or anything that might even remotely allow something, at least, to circulate.

She is not only a good mother, she is also a good seamstress. She has sewn very tightly, as she knows so well how to do. So as not to lose anything.

– Hurry up and swallow that! That's not the only thing I've got to do.

That, is the lumpy mass of potatoes she has cooked as is, steamed, without anything, because with nothing, it's better, with just a little butter.

That, is also the chore of making me eat that lumpy mass of even better potatoes when she already has so much to do . . .

I must help her and make an effort on her behalf, so that this additional work I give might disappear. I, the littlest one, because three children, it's too much.

I must hurry and swallow to make disappear all this even better which clutters the oil-cloth, because that's not the only thing she's got to do, it will also be necessary to clean it.

I don't know where to put them all these potatoes even better with just a little butter. If I spill them, she will begin to yell.

But I can't swallow them either, I already have a digestive

tract full of shit. It has sedimented inside, because of the anus sewn up not to let anything go to waste.

I constantly have stomach ache. It's as hard as concrete. Sometimes the fossilised shit comes back up into my mouth. Then I suck it like a candy.

She does not want me to be.

But she wouldn't want me to be dead either. That would not be enough for her to find peace again.

She wants even less that I should grow up and leave her.

What she wants is that the world should be, like me, never having existed.

To restore grammar to its rights. To write: she wants me to be as not having been.

To give language all its scope. To construct the sentence: 'This woman is my enemy'.

The nutriment she gives me is not for my nourishment. I must not use it to get bigger, grow and become more beautiful, but so that my gratefulness, my gratitude and my thanks increase.

She is a good mother, she has sacrificed herself for us her three children who are her whole life. To digest what she gives would be to insult her. That would mean we want it for ourselves and that we hold back what we should give back.

She only gives food so that the distorting mirror in which she contemplates herself will get fatter. Sending back to her this monstrous image, I disgust myself.

To break this object so that she would stop looking at herself in it. To break it into a thousand shards so that it no longer reflects back the abominable light of totality.

Let living nature integrate this multitude of fragmented fragments into seaweed, trees and batrachians. Let me survive in their midst in the dismemberments of myself. There is no eternal domination.

One day or another I shall be.

'The children' . . .

She talks to me about us, as an indissociable whole, external to me:

– It's necessary to work all the time, to look after the children, go on holidays because of the children, come back and do the washing . . .

There are two hypotheses: either I'm not her daughter or it's not me she's talking to.

I don't know which of the two I prefer.

One day I shall get to the heart of language and denounce the denial of grammar.

– They go bang bang!

We don't know whether she's talking about the police, the soldiers or the militia men, in her mind, armed men, they're all one. And to make sure I fully understand, she specifies:

– With their rifles, they go bang bang!

She can't understand that they belong to the same species as us. She doesn't know the word.

There are they, those who go bang bang, and us, namely her and me who must stay near her because otherwise they go bang bang.

When she utters this sentence, her face changes. Something happens there for which I cannot find any explanation. Nobody has taught me the name of what I see. Facies, symptom, metamorphosis, transfiguration, I don't know the words which would make it possible to tell the fixity of this round dead fish-eyed stare.

In the hospital or the asylum there must exist a technical term.

But here, there is neither ford nor bridge. Language stops at this impassable frontier. One doesn't go through.

– With their guns they go bang bang!

When she says this, she has no fear, she has disappeared.

Nobody can make her understand that there have been victorious revolts in the past.

History doesn't exist.

She repeats to me all the time: 'You cannot remember!'

And yet I remember.

I can't escape as long as I have to look after this mother my father has entrusted to me. He would first have to come and take her back.

Fortunately there's my sister Framboise.* Or Françoise. I don't manage to pronounce the difference.

Besides, her name is Françoise-Annie.

It's not true that what she does to me cannot be told.

She walls me up alive between her re-closed body and the fence of the world to which she forbids me access. I can neither return into her belly nor go away.

* *Framboise* is raspberry. See p. 17 – Trans.

– I no longer remember which one . . .

It's the accepted formula for whatever concerns our childhood. Something happened to one of us two, but to which one . . .

That doesn't matter very much.

In the wordless language of childhood memory, I howl an unfathomable unhappiness. I cannot contain my hiccoughs and sobbing. She runs to close the window and tries to silence me.

– The neighbours will hear you!

But she doesn't manage. She has the same shattered look as when there is water in her kitchen and she stops me going in with an unfriendly 'Don't walk in it'.

She fetches a facecloth, wets it and slaps it on my face.

I can no longer breathe.

The hairs are used to make brushes, the guts ropes and the skin bags. Not to mention meat which one eats, of course! She exults while explaining to me that with a hog everything is salvaged.

It's not the know-how that interests her, it's the mastery. She is very proud of ingeniousness. Her body glows. She all but opens her arms to me.

She is a good housekeeper. In my case, she doesn't waste anything, either. She uses my affection to manipulate me, my clothes to shape my body, my words to kill all hope, my ears to fill them with sand, my mouth to stuff it with herself and my shit to prove our shared anus.

Only my nostrils are of no use to her. It's through these holes that I take in the breath of the world. It has forever the perfume of daffodils.

Her food is prison food. It's not a question of gastronomy or dietetics. These words have no currency. Neither is it a question of feeding us, but of filling us so that no room is left in us where anything other than nutrition, which is her monopoly, could take place. Or rather takes place, for the present indicative is her only conjugation. Not that of the presence hanging between memory and project, but a present of total absence of distance from anything. A defective tense which takes place only where she is. Outside of her there is nothing. And still, in order that there is, and not that there be, there must be a bit of child, food or clothing. Outside of where she has, there is nothing. Food's only function is to fill the emptiness which we are, and nothing else. One would think she is pouring quicklime on corpses.

There is not enough of it for dinner. She does not want me to go to the bakery. She tells me 'Leave the bread for Daddy!'

In the domestic enclosure, through this empty space within this thing of which there is not, I am.

Let whoever is able understand the existence of this hollowed-out world. Between it and the other, I am forever the rubber on the hand which tries to tear me from her womb.

I am the deadest of the dead. Inside the gyneceum, the empty space. Not the nothing, nor the void, the vacancy or the emptiness but the there's not. The most impersonal of what language can produce before going up in smoke.

This spa, where she takes the waters, is boring. I can only go out when she takes a nap. The rest of the time, she doesn't let me go. It's a pity because I like playing Indians with the others. I know how to make bows with hazel-wood. They call me Hawkeye.

I pick up the latest book I just bought, *The Brooklyn Lily*. It's a double volume, it will last me several days. I read peacefully, effortlessly. I would even say that when I am reading I am happy, if this word weren't to be reserved exclusively for time spent with her.

After a few pages, the text is interrupted and I no longer understand what I am reading. I go back and begin again and apply myself. To no avail, there is something abnormal there. Looking at the object more closely, I see that along the spine some cleanly torn-out pages are missing.

I can't believe my eyes.

I reread once more to see if it's not I who, as my mother says 'am imagining things'. Or whether the text is so complicated that I don't understand anything. That would surprise me because with paperbacks it never happens.

The only time was in *Closed Eyes*, a book I was loaned at school. From another collection.

Sometimes the ink is uneven or the text is printed strangely. That doesn't matter. It introduces a bit of fantasy. My mother doesn't like it. That's already something. And in that case, she can't blame me. When books are poorly put together, that happens, pages are badly cut and overhang. But this I have never seen.

I don't understand how it could have occurred . . .

Or rather, since I'm alone with Her, I am really obliged to suspect her. I take my time. I check. Check again. The numbering is categorical. It goes from the leaves on the left to the leaves on the right through an unexplained gap. The numerical sequence is interrupted. My father is right. Mathematics definitely gets the better of literature.

It can only be she who tore the pages from the book. The matter is of great importance, I take my time. I breathe deeply. By inhaling and exhaling, I master the desire I have to throw myself upon her. Breathing alone brings the whole being under control.

Soon, I have no more passion, nor anger nor even cold rage or indignation. Rather, the feeling that those missing pages draw a boundary between her and me at long last.

I do not know the expression 'a demurrer' but I understand it intuitively. The empty space she has created here is forever the site of her negation. Here, where she says there's not, I know that there used to be, and that in ten thousand other copies, there is.

I take my time. I wait for her to come. When she enters the room, I ask her for confirmation.

She makes no secret of what she has done. She is within her maternal prerogatives. Sure of her rights, she explains to me:

– It didn't tally with my philosophy of life.

The wild hope that the book, all by itself, can make murder unnecessary.

'To turn the page.'

She doesn't say 'Let's turn the page', because it would suggest that we have something to do together.

Nor 'Turn the page', because she would be acknowledging that I am suffering and only she and her son are entitled to that verb.

If need be she could say 'You must turn the page', but this 'You' would imply that she is talking to someone, and this someone, oh horrors, could be me.

She says 'To turn the page' as an impersonal formula, except in the expression 'I have always known how to turn the page'.

When she says 'To turn the page', she thinks 'I have always known how to turn the page, what is being said here is a matter of indifference to me.'

'To turn the page', in the infinitive, means that she is not concerned.

To turn the page on her.

The impossibility of having a bond with her. If I tell her about an idea which could involve her, she invariably says:

– That, that's ideas in your head!

Not 'You think that' or 'You have the idea that' but 'ideas in your head', like material things, localised and separate. Without meaning, strictly speaking without links, absurd.

– That, that's ideas in your head!

Ideas in my head. Bearing no relation to me or to the world. She breaks up the foul thing which she has just discovered, in this box placed on her mantelpiece. My head. Separated from me. Besides, of me there is no. Only ideas in my head. Things put away untidily in a box of hers. She notices that she must clean it up. She speaks very softly. It's her fault. She hasn't seen that it was dirty. In my head there are things which should not be there. Fortunately, good housekeeper that she is, she knows how to root them out.

– That, that's ideas in your head!

That. She gathers up into a shapeless magma what I had managed to give shape to. My speech, my effort, my life. That. Everything collusions, coalesces, clings, collates, confusions, sets in a mass, in a place where there is no longer any word. That. She contains me in the unspeakable. In the place where everything melds.

Disorder and night for ever. Not completely. In the blast furnace of nullation where everything is burning, something resists. An unknown matter: some refractory annie, hardening in the fire.

In her an empty space that no one can ever invade, an opening, a passage, breath.

I am condemned to stay beside her in perpetuity. Without having any bond either with her or with the world.

When she unpacks the cheese she says: 'I wrapped it up tightly because it was going to run everywhere, the nasty beast!' I don't hear. I don't listen. A vast hollow is created in the hub of my being. It gets filled with all I read.

My father accuses Dostoevsky of going to my head. He is mistaken, it's Victor Hugo that I prefer: *Hernani* in the Nelson Collection. I declaim the purple passages:

'Mountains of Galicia, Estremadura, Aragon
Oh I have brought misfortune wherever I have gone . . .'

I measure all the accommodations of which the voice is capable. Stronger than the refusal of grammar, there is poetry. Stronger than writing, song. Stronger than inscription, pronunciation.

I also like prose. I have already read the four volumes of *Les Misérables* four times. I know from experience that literature is a lifesaver.

I am condemned to stay beside her in perpetuity. Without having any bond either with her or with the world.

Sh
She
Shhe
Shhh
Shhhhhhh

She swells monstrously in my head and metastasises in the entire language.

I've got forty years.

The nutritious elements of nutrition. The instrument of her organic function.

She proselytises for tasteless food. Boiled potatoes. Vegetable stock. Well-cooked meat. Until everything looks alike: pork, beef and mutton. Still, in this case not quite.

She keeps the blood to pour onto my plate. She knows perfectly well that I don't want any. But by this gesture, she points me out to the assembled family, as the mark of her omnipotence: look how I can tame little Annie!

'Why are you putting blood!' My revolt doesn't make any difference. She is stronger than me. Stronger than the word and the world combined together.

Grammar is useless.

Why are you putting blood?

Her revolt doesn't make any difference. I am stronger than her. Stronger than the word and the world combined. The simple gesture of tipping out the blood makes them all disintegrate. I am she who followeth, the great abolisheress of the eternal, the one who has the knowledge to turn the page of creation.

Father, father, help! I can't breathe any longer. All this blood on the posts of the door of time.

One day, I shall go away, taking in my mouth the unleavened words. The infinitives of the verbs she has not allowed me to conjugate.

I did it in my panties again. I am indeed impossible. I am going to drive her crazy.

In her right hand she holds a wooden spoon, the badge of her command. She plunges it into the stew. Which it does she plunge? It, the mark of her command or it, the spoon?

She plunges ithem into the stew. She stirs grammar up more than she should. Bubbles of chaos come up and burst on the surface.

That monotone voice. That stony timbre without gravity or astonishment. That emission without irritation or humour. That delivery without jolt. That total lack of expressiveness. That speech which puts everything on the same plane, without tenderness or anger, food, things and people.

That flatness ignoring everything about distance, perspective, order or hierarchy. Only permitting itself, when I do not give satisfaction quickly enough, to cut words into absolutely equal segments.

Those sounds, all alike, interchangeable, the one beside the one, proliferating in shapeless and compact groups with no plan other than to invade the whole body. The other's, hers. There's no difference.

Food is the easiest vector. It's the one which penetrates the furthest forward. What is eaten is without danger. You can do it forever and remain the same. That's not true of education.

She does not teach me anything. Especially not to cook. There is not, between her and me, the smallest space where I could grow. She sacrificed herself for us.

How do you say the opposite of a mouth that doesn't want to let go of the breast?

Be that as it may, one of these days I shall have to make up my mind to wean her.

To set up, around her sentences, the cordon sanitaire of inverted commas.

I cannot remember. What?

That it snowed the year I was born? Her jubilation when she recounts that she brandished me in front of her kitchen window? That she put me out, bareheaded on the dormer window-ledge? That icy burn on my uncovered ears?

I cannot remember. What?

The love stories a lady had given me and which she forced me to return. The stiff and shiny paper of the paper covers? That man and that woman stretching towards each other to the point of touching? That new thing so smooth I rubbed it against my cheek?

I cannot remember. What? Dr Soubiran and the *Men in White*?

If I remembered having gathered blue-berry flowers with her and having loved her enough to write about it, I would die.

To turn the page.

To do to her what she has done to me: to erase all traces of her.

Mother spots come off with a bit of writing. Sprinkle generously, starting from the edge. Let stand at least one night. As sorrow comes to the surface, sponge off with clean blotting-paper. Rinse until the water runs clear. Soap normally.

There is no more mummy.

I remain prostrate in the room. Gloom settles into me. I hum shreds of the songs she did not want to teach me. Little by little the shore encroaches upon all the functions of the living. Envelopped in the sands of the bed, I am shielded from the sonars. My torn-off arms half-open again in the midst of the convulsions.

I am lying in the shallows.

In the face of the disaster which she can no longer hide from herself, I hear her lamenting. As an octopus squirts a gush of ink, she utters a nearly-human sentence. You could almost believe she was going to speak directly to me. Faced with her ruined investment, she whines:

– I had placed all my hopes in you . . . What will become of me?

I have broken her toy. I am jubilant.

The wind rises. The storm begins. The sea reaches the borders of the universe. The breath of inspiration unleashes the elements. The waves swell with wild phrases. The metaphors hollow out abysses. The foam sprays enamoured droplets all around.

The language shatters, turned against itself. The hull cracks between resin and acacia. There are no longer birds nor fish. Nothing but the dark flow of the text.

Sinks the skiff, sink the hemp and woollen ribbons. Sink the toys enclosed in the chests. Sinks the food with which they are overburdened. Sinks the sail bearing the bloody ensign of the conquerors.

Sinks to the bottom of the sea, surrounded by the lace, that black Infanta of the corals.

The imputrescible wooden coffin floats empty on the surface of the words.

It is not true that language cannot tell what she does to me.

She never ceases to mingle the child with the mother so that it is as never having been born, never having passed the neck of the womb, never having forced the bolts of the sea.

Holding back each day the birth of the day, she establishes herself out of time, the eternal one abolishing her own creation.

She loves me so much that she does not want to withdraw from me. She wants all of me, and for ever. She loves me as the sun loves the dry grass it ignites. She loves me as the sun loves the proffered fat. She loves me as the sun loves the smoke which rises towards it.

She does not cast a glance towards me. She makes no gesture of compassion. She does not hold out her hand to save me from destruction. She only comments on the tragedy, walling up all that moves with her stony voice:

– 'Granite and silex cannot be dissolved one into the other!'

I burn eternally on her grave to mark its trace.

The ashes of my days rise to the heavens of literature.

Let's turn the page.

I remember Annie Fontaine.